By Norma Simon
ALL KINDS OF CHILDREN
ALL KINDS OF FAMILIES
HOW DO I FEEL?
I AM NOT A CRYBABY!
I WAS SO MAD!
I WISH I HAD MY FATHER
I'M BUSY, TOO
NOBODY'S PERFECT, NOT EVEN MY MOTHER
OH, THAT CAT!
THE SADDEST TIME
WHAT DO I DO? (English/Spanish?)
WHY AM I DIFFERENT?

ALL KINDS OF FAMILIES

By NORMA SIMON   Pictures by JOE LASKER

Albert Whitman & Company • Morton Grove, Illinois

To Margaret Mead

and all my families—N.S.

Library of Congress Cataloging-in-Publication Data
Simon, Norma.
    All kinds of families.
    (A Concept book)
    SUMMARY: Explores in words and pictures what a family is
and how families vary in makeup and lifestyles.
    1. Family—Juvenile literature. [1. Family.]
I. Lasker, Joe. II. Title.
HQ734.S599   301.42   75-42283
ISBN 0-8075-0282-0

Text © 1976 by Norma Simon. Illustrations © 1976 by Joe Lasker.
Published in 1976 by Albert Whitman & Company,
6340 Oakton Street, Morton Grove, Illinois 60053.
Published simultaneously in Canada by General Publishing, Limited, Toronto.
Printed in the United States of America.
30 29 28 27 26 25 24 23 22

About This Book

What does the title of this picture book mean, *All Kinds of Families*?
Quite simply, it acknowledges that families are not always composed
in the traditional way: a household made up of two parents and their
children. The title reflects the many patterns of family life that fit
the broad definition: a group of persons under one roof, usually
subject to one authority or shared authority. It illustrates the family
defined as parents and their children, whether dwelling together or not.

A child defines family on the basis of personal experience. Little
children idealize the adults in their family and learn values by
imitating attitudes and behavior they see around them. This book
stresses the supportive function of the family and the child's joyous
place in the center of this, his world.

Healthy emotional life is nourished by the love, trust, sense of
belonging, and support a family provides. The child also needs
stability, responsiveness, and a pattern of consistency. While many
forms of family structure exist today, the family remains the place
where most children are nurtured, emotionally as well as physically.

This picture book celebrates happy times, but it also shows in a
quiet fashion that some relationships are troubled ones. Separations
and sadness occur, yet the positive values of lives shared endure to
provide foundations for future families.

Norma Simon

A family is YOU. And the people who live with you,
and love you, and take care of you.
There are all kinds of families,
but your own is the one you know best.

Families come in all sizes.
BIG FAMILIES, MIDDLE-SIZED FAMILIES, LITTLE FAMILIES.

Families come in all ages, too.
Young families with young children.
Middle-aged families with teen-aged children.
Old families with grownup children and grandchildren.

Families come with all kinds of people, different sizes,
different ages. They make all kinds of families.

A family is people who belong together.
Like husbands and wives and their children.
Like mothers and children . . . like fathers and children.
Like grandparents and grandchildren.

People who live together, love together, fight together and
make up, work and play with each other, laugh and cry
and live under one roof together . . . They are a family.

What's *special* about a family? It's the feeling you have
about each other from living in the same place,
sharing good times and bad times . . . growing together.

A family can be a mother, a father,
        and children who are growing up.
A family can be a mother and her children,
        living, loving, working and sharing.
A family can be a father and his children,
        living, loving, working and sharing.

A big sister or a big brother
     taking care of other children . . . can be a family.
And a father and a mother together,
     their children grownup and away . . . can be a family.

Children who live far away send letters. They write,
"I'll be home soon.
Can hardly wait to see everybody."

They telephone, too.
"Hi, Mom! Hi, Dad! How are you?
I'll be home for the holidays."

Families like to come together, for holidays, birthdays, a wedding, for sad times and for happy times.

When families get together, they talk a lot, they eat a lot, they laugh a lot.

When everyone has said good-bye, the home feels empty.

Family people have family names.
Like mother, father, sister, brother, son and daughter.
Like cousin, aunt, uncle, niece, nephew,
    grandmother and grandfather.

All your relatives and relations have these family names.

When families go visiting, you hear many family names.
Names like Aunt Susan and Uncle Ed.
Names for different grandparents,
like Grandma Hall and Granny Baker.

Some children have many relatives and relations.
Almost too many to remember.
Some children have only a few, and it's easy
to name every one.

Can you name your aunts?
Uncles? Grandparents?

Do you know their first names?

You are part of your family,

of the caring . . .

and the sharing

and the loving.

From the time when you're a tiny baby,
    when you're growing up . . . all grown up.
All your life, wherever you live,
    YOU are a part of a family.

A family is YOU and the people who live with you. That's one part of your family.

Some people in your family may live in different places. They are still your family.

Part of your family lives far away, in another city . . . in another part of town, or nearby . . . in a different house.

You visit them. They visit you.
And you know that they are family people:
Aunts, uncles, cousins, grandparents.

You are all part of one big family.

A mother or a father may live in a different place,
a place not with their children.
No matter how near or how far, you are still part
of the same family.

Some families live in the same home for a long time.
Other families move from place to place.

But in a family home, there are things people like
    to keep around them: family pictures, a special chair,
        books . . . pets . . . toys.
They take these things from one home to another.

When you are grown up, you may begin your own family,
    a new family . . . a young family.
When a mother and a father have a child or adopt a child,
    a new family begins.

And the *new* family becomes a part
of all the *old* ones:
   Part of the mother's family.
   Part of the father's family.

People in old and new families like to tell each other
where they are, what they are doing.
They send letters, postcards, birthday cards.

Dear Amy,
I wish we could get together more often.
It was wonderful to see you at Thanksgiving.
Thank you for a lovely day.
All the best,
Aunt Ruth

Wish you could come fishing with me
on this beautiful lake.
Yours,
Uncle Jack

Your loving Dad

A kiss and a hug from
Grandma Lucy and Grandpa Bud

A letter for you has YOUR last name on it.

Lots of persons in a family share the same last name.

But, maybe, not all of them.

And some people who aren't even in the same family
have the same last name. That happens!

Families last a long . . . long . . . time.
New babies are born or are adopted.
Some people die.
There are new husbands, new wives . . .
comings together, and goings apart.
There are changes, but families go on.

Families share special stories that family people
like to tell and family people like to hear.

The stories make everyone part of the big family.

Are there stories told in your family?

Maybe there are stories about you, something you did or said?

Maybe you hear the same stories over and over.

Some day . . . you'll tell them, too.

Some uncles tell stories, funny stories, silly stories.
Stories about mischief they did.
Stories about adventures they had.
Stories all about people you know.
And aunts tell you more stories, ones they know.

Families like to tell stories many times.

    The old stories are new to the youngest children.

    They listen and want to hear them again.

Funny stories, sad stories, part of growing up in a family.

Sometimes members of a family
    don't see each other for a long time.
Maybe it's because they live too far away.
Or because families have fights and don't agree.
Maybe people are working,
    and there is no time to be together.

But when a family *does* come together
after a long time, they say things like:
"Oh, how the children have grown!"
"Your hair is still so curly . . ."
"It's *good* to be together again."
"I'd know your girl anywhere.
I remember when you looked like that."
And the family feeling is all around them
        like a strong, invisible circle.

When *you* need help, your family helps you.
When your family needs help, *you* help them.
People in a family help each other
and try to take care of each other.

Yes, families are for caring . . . loving . . . sharing,
far or near, big or little . . . all kinds of families.

All kinds of families—

and yours is one of them.

Your family is always part of you.
You are always part of it.

A family is a special part of your life.

Norma Simon

Books have always been important in her life and so Norma Simon is sensitive to what books can mean to children. Trained in education and psychotherapy, Mrs. Simon writes a special kind of book which reassures children where emotions are concerned. In *I Was So Mad!*, for example, she shows familiar frustrating, anger-provoking situations because she believes the first step in understanding emotions comes when feelings are brought into the open.

While Norma Simon grew up loving the excitement of New York City, she and her family now enjoy the relative peacefulness of life on Cape Cod. In addition to writing, Mrs. Simon works as an educational consultant for advertising research with children and children's products, textbooks, and educational films. She is proud to be a member of her local school committee in Wellfleet, Massachusetts. Her educational background includes undergraduate work at Brooklyn College, graduate work at the New School for Social Research, and a master's degree from the Bank Street School of Education. She has been writing since 1954 and has more than thirty books published. She is a member of the Authors Guild.

Joe Lasker

From the time when he won his first art prize at the age of eight, Joe Lasker knew he wanted to be an artist. He attended the Cooper Union Art School in New York City, but his career was interrupted by service in World War II. When he resumed painting, he won Prix de Rome and Guggenheim fellowships which made possible study in Europe and Mexico. His paintings hang in museums and private collections.

Well known as an illustrator of children's books, Mr. Lasker has become an author as well as artist. His first two picture books, published by Albert Whitman, are *Mothers Can Do Anything* and the sympathetic description of a boy with a learning disability, *He's My Brother.*

Mr. Lasker's illustrations combine strength, a factual realism, and humor. Qualities which enrich his painting make his picture books especially meaningful to anyone involved in the life of girls and boys. His studio is in his home in Norwalk, Connecticut.